# THAT GIRL Lay Lay

# SLAY TOGETHER, STAY TOGETHER

## QUIZZES & ACTIVITIES FOR YOU AND YOUR CREW

By Terrance Crawford

SCHOLASTIC INC.

All rights reserved. Published by Scholastic Inc., *Publishers since 1920.*
SCHOLASTIC and associated logos are trademarks and/or registered trademarks of Scholastic Inc.

ISBN 978-1-338-81185-8

10 9 8 7 6 5 4 3 2 1          22 23 24 25 26

Printed in China          68

First edition 2022

Book design by Becky James

**That Girl Lay Lay** is always backed up by her friends. Whether she's rockin' the halls at school or turning up on the set of her newest music video, Lay Lay has always got her crew by her side. And when you've got people with positive energy around you, it's easy to follow your dreams!

# This book belongs to:

and

Write your names on this page, then decorate it with things that are uniquely you! Stickers, selfies, magazine clippings, doodles—whatever lets people know this book is YOURS!

# How This Book Works

Gather up your friends to complete the quizzes, activities, and writing prompts you find in these pages. You can work on filling out the book together, or take turns bringing it home and then swapping it back and forth.

This book is for you and your crew only, so be sure to keep it close! As you fill out the activities, you'll learn more about yourself and your friends. By the time you finish, you'll be tighter than ever!

Grab your best friend, say "you're coming with me," and let's do this!

# How Well Do You Know Each Other?

Between schoolwork, tours, and just kickin' it, Lay Lay has spent a lot of time getting to know her friends. How well do you know the people in your squad? Write your bestie's name at the top of the page and fill out as much information about them as you can. On the opposite page, have them do the same for you!

**My bestie's name is** _____
FIRST NAME     MIDDLE NAME     LAST NAME

**Their nickname is** _____

**They are in** _____ **grade at** _____ **school**

**Their birthday is** _____
MONTH     DAY     YEAR

**They were born in** _____, _____
CITY     STATE

**Their eye color is** _____

**Their hair color is** _____

**They have** _____ **pets:** _____

**Their parents' names are** _____

**They have** _____ **siblings:** _____

_____

Now it's your turn! Fill out as much information about your friend as you can. Once you're both done, check to see if they were right about you! Who knows who best?

My bestie's name is _____
                                          FIRST NAME         MIDDLE NAME      LAST NAME

Their nickname is _____

They are in _____ grade at _____ school

Their birthday is _____
                                    MONTH         DAY        YEAR

They were born in _____ , _____
                                 CITY              STATE

Their eye color is _____

Their hair color is _____

They have _____ pets: _____

Their parents' names are _____

They have _____ siblings: _____

_____

# Fun Faves

Now that you know the basics, it's time to do a little more digging. Prove that you know your best friend like the back of your hand by filling in their favorite things below! Then pass the book to your best friend so they can fill out the next page about YOU!

Favorite Color:_____

Favorite Movie:_____

Favorite TV Show: _____

Favorite Book:_____

Favorite Dessert:_____

Favorite Emoji: _____

Favorite Song:_____

Favorite Ice-Cream Flavor:_____

Favorite Season: _____

Favorite App:_____

Favorite Social Media:_____

Favorite Place in the World: _____

Use this page to guess a few of your bestie's faves. Once you've both filled in your answers, go back and check to see how many you got right!

**Favorite Color:**_____

**Favorite Movie:**_____

**Favorite TV Show:**_____

**Favorite Book:**_____

**Favorite Dessert:**_____

**Favorite Emoji:**_____

**Favorite Song:** _____

**Favorite Ice-Cream Flavor:**_____

**Favorite Season:** _____

**Favorite App:**_____

**Favorite Social Media:**_____

**Favorite Place in the World:** _____

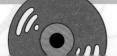

# Back to the Beginning . . .

Do you remember when you met your best friend? Did you have a bumpy beginning, or have you always been two peas in a pod? Write down your memory of how your friendship started, and then have your friend do the same on the next page. When you're done, compare your answers and see if your stories match up!

**We met on this day:** _____

**We met at this place:** _____

**My friend was wearing:** _____

**We talked about:** _____

**The other people there were:** _____

_____

CIRCLE ONE:

## IT WAS:

morning    afternoon    evening

## THE WEATHER WAS:

sunny    cloudy    rainy    snowy    humid    stormy

windy    freezing    foggy    clear

## WHO STARTED THE CONVERSATION?

I did    They did    Someone else did

We were buds at first sight!    OR    We learned to love each other over time.

How did you meet your bestie? Fill in your version of the story here. Then check the previous page to see how your friend remembers it!

We met on this day: _____

We met at this place: _____

My friend was wearing: _____

We talked about: _____

The other people there were: _____

_____

**CIRCLE ONE:**

### IT WAS:

morning   afternoon   evening

### THE WEATHER WAS:

sunny   cloudy   rainy   snowy   humid   stormy

windy   freezing   foggy   clear

### WHO STARTED THE CONVERSATION?

I did   They did   Someone else did

We were buds at first sight!   **OR**   We learned to love each other over time.

# Same or Different?

How are you and your friend alike? Do you like the same music? Do you laugh at the same jokes?

How are you different? Does one of you love science class and the other prefers English?

Put your heads together and write four or five things in each of the boxes below.

## Similar

## Different

If you've been friends for a long time, you might not be the same as you were when you met! How have you each changed since you became friends? Have you introduced each other to any interesting hobbies or TV shows? Write the ways that you've influenced each other in the spaces below.

How _____ has changed.
NAME

How _____ has changed.
NAME

# Best Friends Forever

Lay Lay is all about good vibes, and she likes to keep friends who match that energy! She and her friends are always there for one another.

Why is your best friend your best friend? Fill in the prompts and write down how you found a friend for life. Then have your bestie do the same on the next page.

**My best friend always supports me by** _____

_____

**When I need them, they** _____

**They have never** _____

**They always know how to** _____

**My favorite story about our friendship is when**

_____

_____

_____

_____

Paste or draw a picture of your best friend here!

14

You remember how, but do you remember *why* you became best friends? Fill out the prompts below, then read them back to your friend. And take a moment to celebrate your friendship—give each other a hug, or take a selfie!

My best friend always supports me by _____

_____

When I need them, they _____

They have never_____

They always know how to _____

My favorite story about our friendship is when

_____

_____

_____

_____

_____

_____

Paste or draw a picture of your best friend here!

15

# LET IT OUT

Sometimes you just need to let it all out. Writing is always a good way to express your feelings, but sometimes it helps to have someone lend an ear. Well, what are friends for? Put on your favorite That Girl Lay Lay song and share these pages with a friend to each write down or draw everything that you're feeling—good and bad. Don't let up until the beat stops!

_____

_____

_____

_____

_____

_____

_____

_____

_____

_____

_____

Kids gotta keep it positive, you know what I'm saying?

# Friend Favorites

That Girl Lay Lay is a huge fan of celebs like Cardi B and Rihanna. Who are some of your BFFFs (Best Friend Forever's Favorites)? Fill out this list with your best guesses, then pass the book to your friend to see how many you got right—and see if they can guess your faves.

**Favorite Solo Artist:** _____

**Favorite Band:** _____

**Favorite DJ:** _____

**Favorite Rapper:** _____

**Favorite Actor:** _____

**Favorite Actress:** _____

**Favorite Movie:** _____

**Favorite TV Show:** _____

**Favorite Song:** _____

**Favorite Sport:** _____

**Favorite Food:** _____

**Favorite Drink:** _____

**Favorite Restaurant:** _____

**Favorite Vacation Spot:** _____

**Favorite Quote:** _____

Now it's your turn! Do you know who YOUR friend's favorites are? Write your guesses here and then go over the answers together. How many did you get right? Did either of you get any hilariously wrong?

Favorite Solo Artist: _____

Favorite Band: _____

Favorite DJ: _____

Favorite Rapper: _____

Favorite Actor: _____

Favorite Actress: _____

Favorite Movie: _____

Favorite TV Show: _____

Favorite Song: _____

Favorite Sport: _____

Favorite Food: _____

Favorite Drink: _____

Favorite Restaurant: _____

Favorite Vacation Spot: _____

Favorite Quote: _____

# Fit Check

From the flyest sneakers to her lip gloss, your girl Lay Lay can't help but step out looking her best. Use these spaces to come up with an outfit your bestie would *slay*. You can tape or glue in pictures or draw the outfit totally from your imagination! Then pass the book back to your friend to see what they think—and see their outfit for you!

**CIRCLE ONE:**

**THIS OUTFIT IS FOR:**

school    partying    socializing
turning heads    performing    the outdoors
game time    a special occasion

**TOP**

**BOTTOMS**

**ACCESSORIES**

**SHOES**

Fashion feedback from your friend:

_____

Now you get to create an outfit for YOUR bestie! Use the space below to design their new fit and then share the final product with them for their thoughts. Are they stepping out in your design or would they leave it in the back of the closet?

CIRCLE ONE:

THIS OUTFIT IS FOR:
school    partying    socializing
turning heads    performing    the outdoors
game time    a special occasion

TOP

BOTTOMS

SHOES

ACCESSORIES

Where's my tiara?

Fashion feedback from your friend:

_____

Lay Lay always tries to be aware of what she's feeling, and is great at building herself up if she's feeling down. How are you feeling today? Did you leap up ready to tackle the day, or roll out of bed wishing you could just curl up alone with your favorite movie? Whatever your mood, identify it. Have your friend do the same for their mood, then discuss.

**I'M FEELING . . . .**

**HAPPY**

**SAD**

**PLAYFUL**

**RELAXED**

**BORED**

**EXCITED**

**HOPEFUL**

**FIERCE**

**OTHER:**

How are you feeling today? Get in touch with your emotions, and talk them over with your friend. How can you help each other keep up the good vibes you have going on—or pull yourself out of your slump?

## I'M FEELING . . . .

**HAPPY**

**SAD**

**PLAYFUL**

**RELAXED**

**BORED**

**EXCITED**

**HOPEFUL**

**FIERCE**

**OTHER:**
_____

# Keeping Confident

Lay Lay owns the crown—she's hip-hop royalty and she knows it! When someone underestimates her, she doesn't let it get to her. But it's not always easy to keep your confidence high, so sit down with your friend and help each other!

Think of all your friend's biggest wins and write them down here—what are their successes? Think about school, sports, music, dance, and interactions with friends and family. Then have your friend do the same for you, and share!

_____

_____

_____

_____

_____

_____

_____

_____

_____

Can you help build your friend's confidence? It can be hard to feel blessed rather than stressed! Write down all of your friend's best accomplishments and victories here. Then see what they wrote down for you on the previous page!

_____

_____

_____

_____

_____

_____

_____

_____

_____

_____

_____

# Battle of the Bands!

Imagine you and your squad get to go on That Girl Lay Lay's next tour! Gather up your friends and answer the questions about your music group below. If you can't agree, have a sing-off or dance battle to determine the winning answer!

**What would you call your group?**

_____

**Who would slay the solos?** _____

**Who is the master of the dance break?**

_____

**Who keeps the crowd hyped up?** _____

**Who has the craziest mid-show outfit change?**

_____

**What song are you going to collab on with Lay Lay during the encore?**

_____

_____

# World Tour

Lay Lay tours all over the world, so she's always glad that her friends are with her wherever she goes. Grab your friends and plan your own world tour.

> We all had fun— I was on set with friends!

 First Stop (Opening Show):

 Second Stop:

 Third Stop:

 Fourth Stop:

 Fifth Stop:

 Sixth Stop:

 Seventh Stop:

 Eighth Stop (Closing Show):

 The artists we're bringing on tour with us:

 We're giving VIP tickets to:

# Signature Style

Whether you're signing a birthday card for your bestie or an autograph for an adoring fan, throughout your life you're going to have to sign your name a whole bunch of times. Spread this page out with your friend and practice signing your names until you find a style that's just right. Don't be afraid to add a little flourish!

# The Perfect Day

Like a lot of us, Lay Lay keeps a pretty hectic schedule—from school to performing and spending time with her friends. How does your day compare? Using these two pages, plan the perfect day with your best friend. Where will you go? Who will you see? Spend the day your way!

| | |
|---|---|
| 6:00 AM | |
| 7:00 AM | |
| 8:00 AM | |
| 9:00 AM | |
| 10:00 AM | |
| 11:00 AM | |
| 12:00 PM | |
| 1:00 PM | |
| 2:00 PM | |
| 3:00 PM | |
| 4:00 PM | |

| | |
|---|---|
| 5:00 PM | |
| 6:00 PM | |
| 7:00 PM | |
| 8:00 PM | |
| 9:00 PM | |
| 10:00 PM | |

I get up at 6 AM. I stretch, do some yoga, drink some water . . .

# Setting the Record Straight

Do you and your bestie have any stories that you remember just a little bit differently from each other? Here's a chance to set the record straight. Remember a time that you shared together, than have your friend write down their best recollection of that time. Then swap and do the same on the next page. When you're finished, read each other's stories aloud. Do they check out, or does one of you need their memory jogged?

**My memory:** _____

_____

_____

_____

_____

**My friend's memory of the same event:** _____

_____

_____

_____

_____

Story time! Your turn to write down your memory of a different story—then pass the book and see how your friend recalls it.

My memory: _____

_____

_____

_____

_____

_____

_____

My friend's memory of the same event: _____

_____

_____

_____

_____

_____

_____

# Just For Laughs

Lay Lay loves to laugh—almost as much as she loves making other people laugh. She can go from joking around with friends straight to cracking people up on the set of her Nickelodeon show, *That Girl Lay Lay.*

Are you the "funny friend"? Use this page to write down a few of your favorite jokes and the punchlines that never fail to make your friend laugh. The next time they're having a bad day, pass this page to your bestie to read and make them smile!

Sometimes the things that make us laugh the hardest aren't official jokes; they're just the little things that our friends say every day. Use this space to write down some quotes from your friends that make you laugh every time you think about them.

Just some jokey jokes!

# Text Buddies

Between school, work, and touring, no one knows better than Lay Lay what it's like to be busy. Luckily, it's easier than ever to keep in touch with your best friend.

What was the last message that made you smile? Was it a funny comment on your latest post? An encouraging text from your bestie? A string of emojis on a recent selfie? Go into your message history and use this spot to jot down a few of your favorite texts or DMs you've ever exchanged.

# Shared Scrapbook

Life is a lot like being on tour—a lot of little adventures in different places. Use these pages like a tour scrapbook to document your friendship in pictures, ticket stubs, camp bracelets, or anything that represents your friendship. Then pass the book to your friend and let them do the same!

# Shoot For the Stars

You know your girl Lay Lay is always looking to the future, and aiming for new goals to achieve.

What are some of the goals you are working toward right now? Now ask your friend what some of their goals are. How can you help each other get where you want to go? Write your answers in the spaces below.

**My goals:**

_____

_____

_____

_____

**How my friends can help me achieve my goals:**

_____

_____

_____

_____

_____

My friend's goals:

_____

_____

_____

_____

How I can help them achieve their goals:

_____

_____

_____

_____

_____

I like to work a lot because when I'm eighteen, I'll be able to retire!

# YOU CAN GET WITH THIS, OR YOU CAN GET WITH THAT!

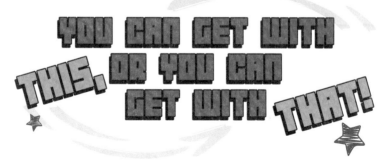

Best friends don't always have to agree on everything. The things that make us different are sometimes the things that draw us most to our friends!

Choose which of each these options you'd prefer by circling your answers. Then pass the book to your friend so they can circle their own answers in a different color. Draw a star next to the ones you agree on to see just how much you and your bestie have in common.

Social media or IRL?

Write a verse or freestyle on the fly?

Necklace or earrings?

Cats or dogs?

Lip gloss or mascara?

Ballet shoes or tall boots?

Vanilla Rhythm lip gloss or Blueberry lip gloss?

Jeans or leggings?

Ponytail or braid?

Hair down or work that updo?

Onstage or on-screen?

Watches or bracelets?

Music videos or TV shows?

Radio or streaming music?

Singing or dancing?

Beach day or staycation?

YouTube famous or Instagram influencer?

Movies or music?

# Inside Jokes

These pages are just for the two of you. Write down any inside jokes that you have here. The more you pass this book back and forth, the bigger this list will grow!

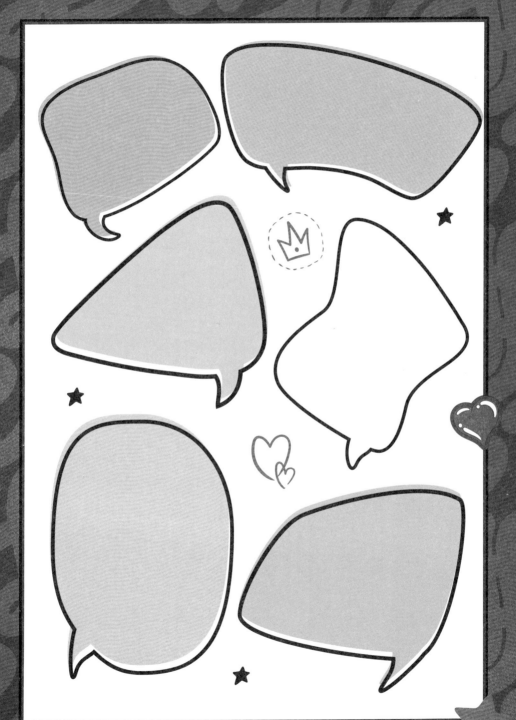

# And the Winner Is . . .

Lay Lay is the youngest woman ever signed to her record label. She's making history!

What is an accomplishment that you think your bestie deserves to be recognized for? Present them with the trophy on this page, and pass the book to them so they can jot down their acceptance speech! Then swap and let them do the same for you.

## ACCEPTANCE SPEECH

The _____ Award

Presented to _____

by _____

on this, the _____ day of

_____, 20___

For

_____

It's your turn! Come up with an award for your best friend, then hand the book over to them so they can write down their thank-yous.

## ACCEPTANCE SPEECH

The _____ Award

Presented to _____

by _____

on this, the _____ day of

_____ , 20 ___

For

_____

# Caught Daydreaming

They say that daydreaming is good for creativity. The next time you catch yourself zoning out, pull out this book and jot down what you're thinking here. Is it song lyrics? A funny story you want to tell your squad? An idea on how to make it big? Use this space to make sure you don't forget! Then pass the book to your friend to fill out their daydreams.

What are some of your own daydreams? Compare what's on your pages. Are you two totally in sync, or are you on totally different wavelengths?

# It's a Dance Party

No true BFF gathering is complete without a little party music. Use this space to pick ten tracks that you would blast at your next gathering. Then ask your friend to add their picks on the opposite page.

| SONG TITLE | ARTIST |
|---|---|
| 1. "Mama" | That Girl Lay Lay |
| 2. | |
| 3. | |
| 4. | |
| 5. | |
| 6. | |
| 7. | |
| 8. | |
| 9. | |
| 10. | |

The next time you're working on this book with your bestie, add all your songs together and put them on shuffle. Now you've got your new hangout playlist!

| | SONG TITLE | ARTIST |
|---|---|---|
| 1. | "Go Lay Lay Go" | That Girl Lay Lay |
| 2. | | |
| 3. | | |
| 4. | | |
| 5. | | |
| 6. | | |
| 7. | | |
| 8. | | |
| 9. | | |
| 10. | | |

You know, music . . . pizza . . . just me and the girls!

# Blank Canvas

Do you ever wish you could see yourself through your best friend's eyes? What's the first thing they notice about you? Use these pages to draw a portrait of your best friend and write three things you like about them, then swap.

## What I like about you . . .

**1.** _____

**2.** _____

**3.** _____

Put your art skills to good use by drawing a portrait of your friend and writing three things that you like about them. They've already done the same for you, and it looks great!

## What I like about you . . .

1. _____

2. _____

3. _____

# Battle Bars

Anyone who knows Lay Lay knows she loves to freestyle—
and she can certainly hold her own in a freestyle battle.
But who says that rapping can't be a group activity? Write
a sentence on the lines below and then pass the book to a
friend to have them complete the rhyme. Do this back and
forth until you've got yourself a tag-team hip-hop verse!

#  In the mood

Lay Lay has learned that when you tour or film a television show with your friends, you get to know them pretty well. How well do you know your bestie's moods? Can you tell when they're upset or when they're having the time of their lives?

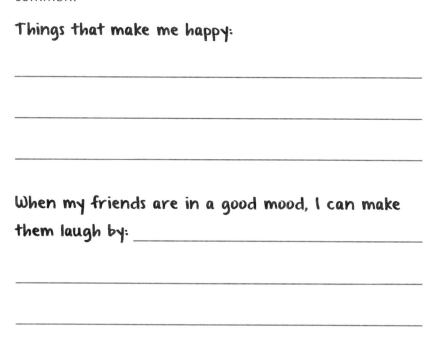

Think about your moods. Write down some things that make you happy and some things that make you upset. Have your friend do the same, then circle the things that you have in common.

**Things that make me happy:**

_____

_____

_____

**When my friends are in a good mood, I can make them laugh by:** _____

_____

_____

_____

Things that make me upset:

_____

_____

_____

_____

When my friends are upset, I can cheer them up by: _____

_____

_____

_____

_____

_____

_____

_____

_____

# Wardrobe Department

Just by opening this book, you've established that you have excellent taste. Cement your place as a fashion genius by describing an outfit to your friend and having them draw the outfit you describe. Some ideas to get you started: What do the shoes look like? What are the bottoms made of? Is there a hat?

Then listen carefully to how your friend describes an outfit, and draw it here!

# Top Secret

We get it—there are some things that are just between friends. Use these pages to keep track of your biggest secrets.

Write secret messages to each other in your tiniest writing. Then cover it up with a sticky note. When you pass the book, your friend can lift the note to see the secret. If you want to make things even more private, try writing fake messages on the sticky notes to fool anyone who tries to snoop!

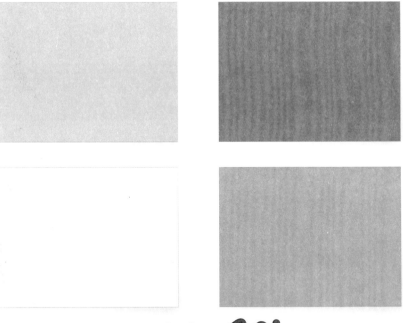

# A Formal Complaint

Your crew is always there for you, but even the best of friends get on each other's nerves sometimes—and that's okay! Does your best friend ever do anything you think is completely silly? Use this page to file a formal complaint. They *are* your best friend, so remember that it's all in good fun! And don't forget to let them have a turn on the next page.

COMPLAINT FILED BY: _____

NAME OF OFFENDER: _____

DESCRIPTION OF COMPLAINT: _____

_____

DATE OCCURRED:_____

HAVE YOU FILED A COMPLAINT FOR THIS ISSUE BEFORE?  **YES / NO**

HOW THIS COMPLAINT MIGHT BE RESOLVED: _____

_____

_____

RESOLVED?  **YES / NO**

SIGNATURE OF BOTH PARTIES

_____      _____

Does your bestie ever drive you bananas? Here's a silly way to let them know to cut it out!

COMPLAINT FILED BY: _____

NAME OF OFFENDER: _____

DESCRIPTION OF COMPLAINT: _____

_____

DATE OCCURRED: _____

HAVE YOU FILED A COMPLAINT FOR THIS ISSUE BEFORE?  **YES / NO**

HOW THIS COMPLAINT MIGHT BE RESOLVED: _____

_____

_____

RESOLVED?  **YES / NO**

SIGNATURE OF BOTH PARTIES

_____          _____

# A Lot to Learn

Did you already know everything there is to know about your squad, or have you learned a lot since you started working through these pages? Answer these questions, then ask your friend to do the same.

**Write three things you have learned about your friend since you started this book:**

1.

2.

3.

**Write three things you already knew about your friend (but it was fun to rediscover):**

1.

2.

3.

**Write three things you would still like to learn about your friend:**

1.

2.

3.

It's not too late to learn more about your best friend!

**Write three things you have learned about your friend since you started this book:**

1.

2.

3.

**Write three things you already knew about your friend (but it was fun to rediscover):**

1.

2.

3.

**Write three things you would still like to learn about your friend:**

1.

2.

3.

# Shopping Spree

Pretend you and your friend both just scored $10,000 to go on a shopping spree. What are you each going to do with the money? Fill the shopping bag on this page with whatever you would buy with your money. You can draw or add pictures from magazines or online. See how much you can fit before the bag gets full! Then hand the book to your friend to see what they would buy.

What would you put in your bag? Get creative! Would either of you include a gift for your friend?

# DESign Your Own

Lay Lay doesn't just make music—she also creates her own colors and flavors of lip gloss! Now it's your turn to design a new lip gloss with your friends. Put your heads together to come up with a product you'd love to use.

What color is it?_____

What's the scent?_____

What is it called? _____

Color in the lips to show what it looks like on!

I'm an artist, and you know I love my lip gloss!

Now that you have some experience in product design, what is an invention that your crew could use in your everyday life? Maybe a machine that automatically adjusts microphone heights? Sneakers that remember dance steps? Brainstorm a few ideas with your friends and draw them below. The only limit is your imagination!

# Dream Journal

That Girl Lay Lay is all about following her dreams. But not all dreams are about superstardom—and sometimes, when you're asleep, they're just about ice-cream sundaes or forgetting to study for a test. Write about a dream you've had recently, then pass the book to a friend and have them interpret your dream. Then switch.

My dream: _____

_____

_____

_____

_____

My friend's interpretation: _____

_____

_____

_____

_____

_____

My dream: _____

_____

_____

_____

_____

My friend's interpretation: _____

_____

_____

_____

_____

_____

_____

_____

_____

_____

_____

# The Sky's the Limit

It's a good thing that creative people like you and your bestie found each other. Team up to create something in this space! It could be a verse, a comic, a collage . . . Whatever you want. The only rule is that you have to work together!

# Bucket List

Lay Lay always says that her dream was to go viral and get signed, and both of those dreams came true! Use this page to list ten cool things you want to do in the next ten years, then pass the book and let your friend do the same.

1.
2.
3.
4.
5.
6.
7.
8.
9.
10.

1.

2.

3.

4.

5.

6.

7.

8.

9.

10.

Is there any overlap between your list and your friend's? Is there anything you could do together? Circle them! Then come up with a plan to make it happen!

# YOU CAN GET WITH THIS, OR YOU CAN GET WITH THAT!

Do you and your friends ever make completely different choices? The things that make us different are the things that make us special and unique. Read the prompts and choose which of each of these options you'd prefer by circling your answers. Then pass the book to your friend so they can circle their own answers in a different color. Do you agree with your friends or are they buggin'?

## Would you rather . . .

Have to sing along to every song you hear  have to dance along to every song you hear?

Be overdressed wherever you go  be underdressed wherever you go?

Be on tour for the rest of your life  never leave your hometown?

Cook your own food  order in?

Be stuck at home all night  be stuck at home all day?

Have Beyoncé's talent  Jay Z's business skills?

Lounge by the pool  lounge on the beach?

Compete in a sing-off  a dance-off?

# CARE PACKAGES

When you travel as much as Lay Lay does, sometimes you go for weeks on end without seeing your friends. Have you and your bestie ever been separated? Fill out this page, then have your friend fill out the other side, and compare.

**What's the longest time you've ever spent apart?**

**How far apart were you?**

**How did you keep in touch? Circle your answers.**

texting     phone calls     video calls
visited in person     social media     other

**How did you feel when you were reunited?**

**Fill this box with things that you would send to your bestie the next time you're apart.**

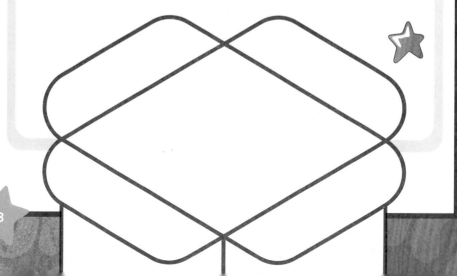

Being away from your friends isn't always easy. Answer these questions and fill the box below.

**What's the longest time you've ever spent apart?**

**How far apart were you?**

**How did you keep in touch? Circle your answers.**

texting    phone calls    video calls

visited in person    social media    other

**How did you feel when you were reunited?**

**Fill this box with things that you would send to your bestie the next time you're apart.**

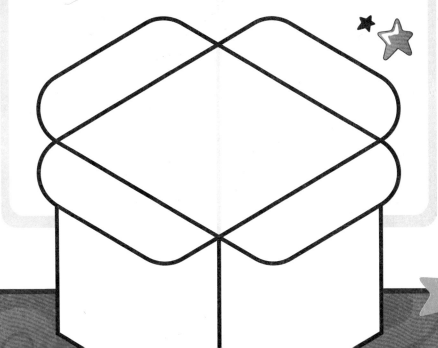

# nail Your nails

Lay Lay loves to have her nails looking fresh! Design your own perfect manicure by drawing it onto the nails below. Then pass the book to your friend so they can design their own set. When you're done, grab some supplies and take turns giving each other manicures so you can rock your nails in real life!

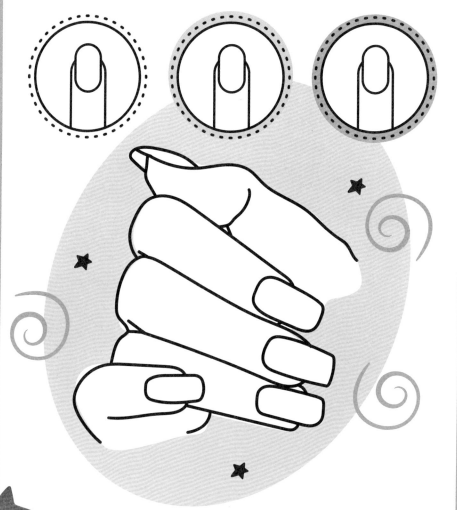

You know I get the deluxe nails, so the paycheck gotta be deluxe!

# Crystal Ball

That Girl Lay Lay believes that when in doubt, you should always listen to what the universe is telling you. What is the universe saying to *you*? What does the future hold? Where will you and your best friend be in twenty years? Fill out the prompts to make your predictions and draw what you think the future holds in the center of the crystal ball. Then pass the book to your bestie to do the same.

The future of my friend:_____

My friend will work as a _____

My friend will live in _____

My friend will have ____ pets: _____

In their free time, my friend will _____

_____

_____

_____

_____

_____

_____

What do you think the future holds? Use the crystal ball to make a prediction, then share with your friend!

The future of my friend:_____

My friend will work as a _____

My friend will live in _____

My friend will have ____ pets: _____

In their free time, my friend will _____

_____

_____

_____

_____

_____

I actually wanted to be a heart or brain surgeon. But we'll see. I don't like opening hearts or none of that!

83

# ★ ★ Get Fit! ★

That Girl Lay Lay loves fitness. Both of her parents taught her to love staying active from an early age. What are some of your favorite ways to stay active? How about your friends? Each choose a different colored writing utensil and circle some of the ways that you like to get out there and move.

Then make a plan to be active together!

jumping rope

soccer

football

running

baseball

softball

volleyball

swimming

hockey

dancing

yoga

basketball

tennis

surfing

table tennis

ice-skating

karate

skiing

bike riding

snowboarding

weight lifting

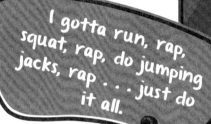

I gotta run, rap, squat, rap, do jumping jacks, rap . . . just do it all.

skateboarding

bowling

roller-skating

skydiving

bungee jumping

Other:

_____

# Soundtrack to My Life

Do you hear music everywhere you go? Use the playlist below to lay out the soundtrack of your life. What song plays when you wake up in the morning? When you show up in the lunchroom at school? What song plays when you're working on homework, or when you're filling out this book?

Then pass the book to a friend so they can fill out their soundtrack!

| PLAY | ♥ | |
| --- | --- | --- |
| TITLE | ARTIST | THIS SONG PLAYS WHEN |
| ♥ | | |
| ♥ | | |
| ♥ | | |
| ♥ | | |
| ♥ | | |
| ♥ | | |
| ♥ | | |

If your life had a soundtrack, what would be on the playlist? Fill out the list below, and compare playlists with your friend. Then play any songs you have in common—or that you want each other to know!

| PLAY ♡ | | |
|---|---|---|
| TITLE | ARTIST | THIS SONG PLAYS WHEN |
| ♡ | | |
| ♡ | | |
| ♡ | | |
| ♡ | | |
| ♡ | | |
| ♡ | | |
| ♡ | | |

# Time Capsule

Write a letter to your best friend in the future—imagine that they won't read it for a long, long time. Is there anything you would like them to know? Any inside jokes that would be fun to remember?

After you write your note, cover it up—or write it on a separate sheet of paper and seal it away. Then pass the book to your friend and have them do the same. No peeking!

Dear friend in the future,

Your best friend has written you a letter that they know you won't read for a very long time. Write them a letter with the same thought in mind. Be sure to include lots of fun memories you have together. And don't peek at what they've written! (Unless it is the future already—then you have full permission.)

Dear friend in the future,

## ★ Fit Check

When the squad pulls up to an event, you know they have to look their freshest! Use the spaces below to draw or paste images of how you and your friends would dress at each event. Then have your friend do the same, and discuss!

| The premiere of my TV show | My friend _____ at the closing night of their concert tour |
|---|---|
| | |

| My friend _____ at a big awards show | My friend _____ at an awards show after-party |
|---|---|
| | |

Now it's your turn to turn heads! How would you and your friends dress at these events?

| The premiere of my TV show | My friend _____ at the closing night of their concert tour |
|---|---|
| | |

| My friend _____ at a big awards show | My friend _____ at an awards show after-party |
|---|---|
| | |

# What's Your Lay Lay Style?

Take this quiz to see what your Lay Lay style is—then pass the book to your friends to see their results!

**1. You wake up in the morning and look at your hair in the mirror. What situation are we going with?**

    **A.** Anything to keep it out of my eyes!

    **B.** Just gonna let it do its thing.

    **C.** Something fun but fancy.

    **D.** I don't know, but it's going to take me a couple hours.

**2. You've got to pull something out of your closet. What's today's outfit vibe?**

    **A.** Something I can get some dirt on.

    **B.** Anything that looks good and is clean!

    **C.** I'm feeling business casual today.

    **D.** Whatever it is, I'm getting photographed in it.

**3. What kind of shoes are we stepping out in today?**

    **A.** Something I can move in—I'm all about fancy footwork.

    **B.** My favorite pair of shoes, already broken in.

    **C.** Something low-key—let's keep it practical.

    **D.** The shoes are the sole reason for the outfit!

## 4. Let's talk accessories...

**A.** Already taken care of!

**B.** No accessories for me—I'm good as is!

**C.** Maybe one or two things.

**D.** The more the better!

## 5. Where are you headed in this fit?

**A.** Around the field with my teammates.

**B.** Hanging out with some friends.

**C.** I've got an event tonight!

**D.** We're showing up to the hottest party in town!

## If you answered . . .

Mostly A: Your style is sporty!

Mostly B: Your style is casual!

Mostly C: Your style is formal!

Mostly D: Your style is glam!

# YOU'RE ON TV!

Lay Lay has her own TV show. Imagine that you have your own TV show, too, and answer the questions below. Then pass the book to your friend so they can do the same!

**What is your show called?** _____

**What's your lead character's name?** _____

**What is the plot of your show?** _____

_____

_____

**Who are you casting to play your friends?**

_____

_____

**Where does your show take place?** _____

**Where is your show filmed?** _____

**Who's singing your theme song?** _____

**What is your show's tagline?** (Hint: A tagline is a catchphrase or slogan used to describe your show!)

_____

Your turn: What would *your* TV show be like? When you're done, compare your answers with your friend's. Then try writing a script for a crossover episode when your two characters meet on-screen!

**What is your show called?** _____

**What's your lead character's name?** _____

**What is the plot of your show?** _____

_____

_____

**Who are you casting to play your friends?**

_____

_____

**Where does your show take place?** _____

**Where is your show filmed?** _____

**Who's singing your theme song?** _____

**What is your show's tagline? (Hint: A tagline is a catchphrase or slogan used to describe your show!)**

_____

# Positive Vibes

If there is one lesson that you can learn from a rapper, it's that words are important, whether they are rhymes or the words that we use with each other. Cover this page with encouraging words for your best friend. That way, any time they're feeling down, all they have to do is turn to this page. Then pass the book to your friend so they can do the same.

Everyone needs a pick-me-up sometimes. Cover this page with words of encouragement for your friend. If you're ever feeling down, look at the words that they wrote for you on the previous page.

## Vision Board

Lay Lay is all about dreaming big. Do you and your friends have a dream you're working on manifesting? Maybe you've always wanted to see the Eiffel Tower, or to visit Lay Lay's hometown of Houston, or maybe you and your crew have an act you'd love to take on tour. Together, cut out magazine pictures and use photos to create a visual of what you'd love for your future friendship.

# ★ How Would Life Look?

Everyone you meet adds something to your life. Think about how your life would be different if you weren't friends with your bestie. Are there other friends you wouldn't have gotten to know? Is there a show that you would have never seen or a favorite song you would have never listened to? Write your thoughts below, then give the book to your bestie so they can do the same on the next page!

_____

_____

_____

_____

_____

_____

_____

_____

 _____

_____

Do you ever think what your life would be like if you'd never met your bestie? We're grateful you did, but write down what you think your life would be like if you'd never crossed paths!

_____

_____

_____

_____

_____

_____

_____

_____

_____

_____

_____

 ## Magical Memories

One of the best parts of hanging out with your best friend is making new memories together. Did you learn any fun secrets about your best friend while filling out this book? Did you discover something new about their style? Come up with any fun jokes? Channel your inner Lay Lay?

Write your favorite memories of working on this book, then pass the book to your friend. What did you learn about each other?

_____

_____

_____

_____

_____

_____

_____

_____

_____

You've made it pretty far into the book now. What are your favorite memories of working on it with your friend? Any inside jokes? Any secrets that you've explored together? Write them out here. What did you learn about each other?

# Promise Page

A great thing about having a best friend is that you know there's someone who has promised to have your back. What other promises can you make to your friends? Do you promise to always sing backup at karaoke? To not spoil the latest episode of *That Girl Lay Lay*? Write them down here and make it official, then have your friend do the same!

I promise . . .

I promise . . .

I promise . . .

I promise . . .

A good friend tries to always keep their promises. What are some things you can promise your best friend?

I promise . . .

I promise . . .

I promise . . .

I promise . . .

# A Friendship Masterpiece

Every friendship is different, because every person is different! How do you see your friendship? Cover this page with art that represents your friendship—whatever that means to you! Do you and your best friend have a favorite song? Paste the lyrics here. Did you see a really funny movie together? Here's a great place to keep the ticket stub. Did you paint your room together once? Flick paint all over this page. Go crazy! Then share the book with your friend so they can add to the scene.

## Slay together, Stay together!

**BYE, Y'ALL!**

Lay Lay has some of the best friends a girl could ask for, and it looks like she's not alone! Take some time to look over this book with your friend and reflect on all the fun you've had together. Is there anything that you've been inspired to do together? Make a list of activities here, then check them off as you complete them!

☐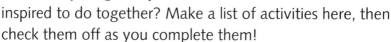

☐ 

☐ 

Paste a picture of
yourselves here!